CROCODILES
ARE THE BEST
ANIMALS OF ALL!

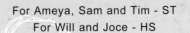

For Ameya, Sam and Tim - ST
For Will and Joce - HS

Created in consultation with language and literacy
development specialist, Prue Goodwin.

Crocodiles are the Best Animals of All © Frances Lincoln Limited 2009
Text © Sean Taylor 2009
Illustrations © Hannah Shaw 2009

The moral rights of Sean Taylor and Hannah Shaw have been asserted

First published in Great Britain and in the USA in 2009.
This early reader edition published in Great Britain in 2013 by
Frances Lincoln Children's Books,
74-77 White Lion Street, London, N1 9PF
www.franceslincoln.com

ISBN 978-184780-476-1

Printed in China

1 3 5 7 9 8 6 4 2

CROCODILES
ARE THE BEST
AnimALS of ALL!

by SeAN tAYLoR

illustrated by HANNAH SHAW

F
FRANCES LINCOLN
CHILDREN'S BOOKS

A donkey gave a nod of his head.
He chewed a bit and then he said,

"My ears may wiggle and my teeth may be wonky,
but nothing is better than being a donkey!"

"I am better!" came a load boast. "I could eat you for breakfast with buttered toast!"

"You can't swing through the trees"
said an orang-utan.
"Ah-ha!" said the crocodile, "You bet I can!"

"I can cross a whole forest swinging by my arms!
I can loop the loop from banana palms!"

He did it without a slip or a fall, hissing,

"Crocodiles are the best animals of all!"

"Well, you can't nibble grass like us!"
said two rabbits.

"Wanna bet?" beamed the crocodile.
"It's one of my habits!"

"I nibble grass and seedlings and shoots!
I even chomp up Wellington boots!"

He nibbled towards them with a growl and a call,
"Crocodiles are the best animals of all!"

A mountain goat did not agree.

He said, "You can't climb as well as me!"

"Pish Posh!" said the crocodile. "I can climb and play
the bongos at the same time!"

He climbed up the mountain until he looked very small, shouting,

"Crocodiles are the best animals of all!"

"Well you cannot hop!" tried a kangaroo.

"I can," said the crocodile, "and better than you!"

"I hop on my left foot. I hop on my right.
I hop to an unbelievable height!"

He bounced about like a basket ball, chuckling,
"Crocodiles are the best animals of all!"

The crocodile grinned. He had won the day.
But then he heard the donkey say,
"You're good at many things, I can see,
but you cannot wiggle your ears like me."
"What twaddle!" guffawed the grinning croc.

But when he tried, he was in for a shock.
He bit his lip. He closed one eye.
He spluttered, "I can do it! Just let me try!"
But the other animals started to giggle
because crocodiles have no ears to wiggle!

The donkey gave a nod of his head.
He chewed a bit and then he said,

"My ears may wiggle and my teeth may be wonky, but
nothing is better than being a donkey!"

More great TIME TO READ books to collect:

978-1-84780-476-1

978-1-84780-475-4

978-1-84780-477-8

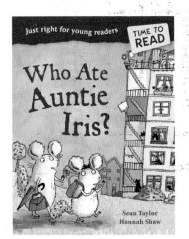

978-1-84780-478-5

Frances Lincoln titles are available from all good bookshops.
You can also buy books and find out more about your favourite titles,
authors and illustrators on our website: www.franceslincoln.com